I Can Read!

BEGINNING
1
READING

The Berenstain Bears
and
MAMA FOR MAYOR!

Jan & Mike Berenstain

HARPER
An Imprint of HarperCollins*Publishers*

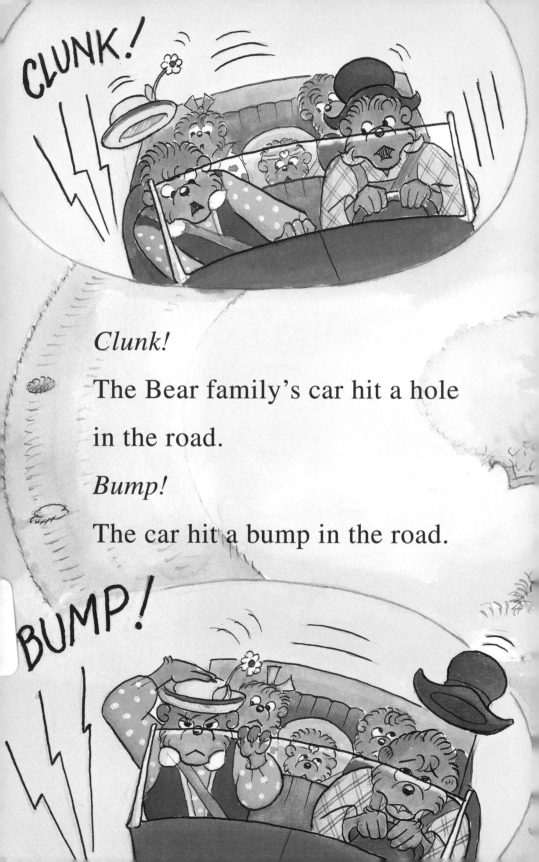

Clunk!

The Bear family's car hit a hole
in the road.

Bump!

The car hit a bump in the road.

"Someone should do something about this road,"
said Mama.
"Yes," said Papa. "But who?"

Back home, Mama
thought and thought.

"I know what to do to fix the road," she said. "I will run for mayor!"

"Good idea," said Papa.

"Hooray!" cried the cubs.

"Mama for mayor!"

So Mama went to the town hall
to sign up to run for mayor.
Papa, Brother, Sister, and Honey
went with her.
They were going to help her run for mayor.

The whole family made posters that said "Mama for mayor."

They put them up around town.

The family made buttons, shirts, and hats
that said "Mama for mayor."
They put them on and wore them
around town.

Papa put up signs on their car.

He drove around town shouting

"Mama for mayor!"

13

All the bears running for mayor
went to the town hall.
They gave speeches.
Mama listened to the speeches.
She thought they were
pretty boring.

Mama gave her speech.

She said she would fix the roads.

Everyone cheered.

She said she would put up

new streetlights.

Everyone cheered.

GO MAMA!

YES!

AWESOME!

YEA!

Mama liked it when everyone cheered.

She said she would get the trash

picked up.

Everyone cheered.

"Dear," whispered Papa, "maybe you are

saying too much."

But Mama went right on.

YEA! YEA!

Mama said there would be honey
in every pot.
She said there would be salmon
in every stream.
All the bears cheered and stomped
and whistled.
"Mama for mayor!" they shouted.

MAMA FOR MAYOR!

The day to vote soon came.

Mama and Papa voted early.

So did the other bears running for mayor.

Mama went to The Burger Bear
for breakfast.
She shook hands.
She kissed babies.
She posed for pictures.

Mama, Papa, and the cubs went home.

They waited for the votes to be counted.

Later, they heard shouting outside.

"Hooray!" they heard. "Mama wins!"

Mama was the new mayor of Bear Country.

She went to sleep very happy.

But the next morning,

Mama was not so happy.

There was a big crowd

outside the tree house.

They were angry.

They carried signs and shouted.

"Fix the road!" they shouted.

"Put up streetlights!" they yelled.

"Pick up the trash!" they called.

They wanted Mayor Mama to do
all the things she said she would—
right now!

"There is just one thing wrong with running for mayor," said Brother. "You just might win!"